"He confessed!" squeaked Mort.

The mice gasped and gawked at each other in horror.

"Guilty!" shouted Mikey, waving the knife. "Guilty! Guilty!"

Salem's head snapped back toward them. "It's only a toy," he protested.

"He adds insult to injury!" shrilled Mikey.

Mort crossed his tiny arms and looked sternly at Salem. "Cat, we find you guilty of the murder of Moto-Mouse. Are you ready to suffer your just punishment?"

"Punishment?" sneered Salem. "Right. What do you pipsqueaks think you can do to me?"

With that, Mikey swung the white plastic blade menacingly back and forth in front of Salem's nose. "We're going to do to *you* what you did to our pal Moto!"

Sabrina, the Teenage Witch™
Salem's Tails™

Available from POCKET Books

All Pocket Book titles are available by post from:
Simon & Schuster Cash Sales, P.O. Box 29, Douglas, Isle of Man IM99 1BQ
Credit cards accepted. Please telephone 01624 836000,
Fax 01624 670923, Internet http://www.bookpost.co.uk
or email: bookshop@enterprise.net for details

KITTY CORNERED

David Cody Weiss and Bobbi JG Weiss

Based upon the characters in Archie Comics

And based upon the television series
Sabrina, The Teenage Witch
Created for television by Nell Scovell
Developed for television by Jonathan Schmock

Illustrated by Mark Dubowski

POCKET
BOOKS

LONDON · SYDNEY · NEW YORK

POCKET
BOOKS

An imprint of Simon & Schuster UK Ltd
Africa House, 64-78 Kingsway
London WC2B 6AH

POCKET BOOKS and colophon are registered
trademarks of Simon & Schuster
A CIP catalogue record for this book is
available from the British Library

ISBN 0 671 77336 4

1 3 5 7 9 10 8 6 4 2

Printed and bound in Great Britain
by Omnia Books Ltd, Glasgow

To NEWT.
We miss you.

"I'd like to place an order. . . . I'll be paying with cash. . . . First item, mouse on a string—now that's a real mouse, right? . . . Oh, well, I'll take it anyway."

—*Salem*

KITTY CORNERED

Chapter 1

"Mmmlphgg?" gulped Salem Saberhagen. He was crouched over his food bowl in the Spellman kitchen, his mouth stuffed with cat chow.

Sabrina Spellman's voice echoed down the hallway, followed by the sound of her approaching footsteps. "I said, don't you dare eat all your food as soon as I walk out the door—like *last* time."

Looking more like a chipmunk collecting for a long winter than a house cat,

Salem tried to swallow the evidence of his guilt all at once. Crunching and gulping, he ran away from the scene of the crime. His claws scrabbled on the slick linoleum surface of the floor as Sabrina's footsteps grew louder.

Salem jumped for the top of the kitchen's center island and would have landed gracefully if his overstuffed belly hadn't clipped the edge. *Whoofing* at the impact, he dug his claws into the wood and pulled himself upright. He froze in a standard bored cat pose just as Sabrina walked in. His attitude of innocence was spoiled only by a quick grimace of pain as he swallowed the last dry kibble crumbs he'd stuffed in his cheeks.

Sabrina stared at Salem's watering eyes with concern. "Are you all right?" she asked.

"I'm . . . heartbroken at being left behind while everyone else runs off."

2

"Oh, give me a break," groaned Sabrina, putting her hands on her hips.

Salem frowned, annoyed that nobody ever believed him when he was trying to fool them. "Seriously," he said, trying to sound hurt, "why am I always the one who gets left behind when it comes to going out and having fun?"

Sabrina pointed her index finger at the counter. Sparks burst from her fingertip, and a small mirror appeared, floating in midair in front of Salem's face.

Although Sabrina Spellman looked and acted like a normal teenage girl, she was in fact a witch with magical powers. A half-witch, actually, since her father was a witch but her mother was an ordinary human. Zapping mirrors out of thin air was one of the good things about being able to use magic. "Okay," she said to the cat, "what part of this reflection don't you understand?"

3

Salem cocked his head, studying himself in the mirror. "Well, I could use a diamond-studded collar and a gold tag proclaiming me King of the Cats, but otherwise . . . boy, am I one gorgeous feline!"

"That's right," said Sabrina. "The last part, anyway. You're a *cat*. A house cat, in fact. And your job is to stay *in the house*. It's part of your sentence."

At the word *sentence,* Salem slumped. He hadn't always been a cat. Once he had been a warlock, and a powerful one, too. But his ego had made him think that he should be the rightful ruler of the mortal world. When he was caught trying to conquer the globe, the Witches' Council had stripped him of his powers and sentenced him to a hundred years in the form of a cat. Sabrina's aunts, Zelda and Hilda Spellman, were assigned to take

4

care of him and to see that he behaved during his sentence.

"Being punished is no reason not to be allowed to have fun," Salem objected.

"Who's having fun?" Sabrina asked. "Aunt Hilda is in Switzerland at a cuckoo clock auction. That's work. And Aunt Zelda's at the 'Brew-Ha-Ha XXX,' the annual Potions Convention in the Other Realm. She's giving a lecture on 'Poultry Potions: Chicken Soup as a Brewing Base.' That's work, too."

"But you're going on a field trip," Salem pointed out. "With Harvey. Try telling me there's no fun in that."

"If it were just him and me alone in the country, maybe," Sabrina objected. "But when it's Principal Kraft taking our science class to a farm to watch manure being turned into a fuel source— ewww."

Try as he might, Salem couldn't help but wrinkle his own nose at the thought.

"Hey, that reminds me," said Sabrina. "I almost forgot my clothespin." She pointed her finger, and a plastic clothespin appeared in her hand. Gently she clipped it onto her nose. "It's either dis or gib myself a twenty-four-hour head code."

Satisfied with the fit, Sabrina pointed again. The clothespin magically removed itself from her nose and floated into her purse.

Then the teenage witch looked sternly at her house cat. "I'm warning you again before I go," she said. "Don't eat all your food as soon as I walk out the door."

"But it's natural," complained Salem. "Cruel Nature forced my feline ancestors to eat whenever they could because they never knew when their next meal would be."

"Excuse me, but you don't have any feline ancestors," Sabrina pointed out dryly. "You're just a witch in the shape of a cat."

"All the more reason to forage when I can," Salem smugly insisted. "More than the natural cat, I am forced to depend on my instincts just to survive!"

Sabrina wasn't buying any of it. "If so, then your instincts seem to be on vacation. Aunt Hilda got her credit card bill yesterday, and it shows six charges for deliveries from the Sharper Kitty Catalog. What do you say to that?"

Salem didn't twitch a whisker. "I haven't touched her credit card since that tuna farm franchise mishap."

Sabrina remembered that mess all too well. Yuck, the smell had been awful! "Salem, you should have known that you can't raise tuna in a bathtub."

"I wouldn't have had to resort to such

7

drastic measures if one of the witches in this house would zap me a proper koi pond!" Regaining his composure, Salem licked a paw. "It served you guys right when the tuna escaped and wound up in every room of the house. You're lucky I was around to hunt down and eat every one." He closed his eyes and smacked his chops at the tasty memory.

"Oh, the pure-hearted sacrifices you make for the good of us all," teased Sabrina. Then she narrowed her eyes. "So you're *sure* you didn't take Aunt Hilda's card again?"

"I didn't have to. I memorized the number."

"Salem—!"

A car honked loudly in front of the Spellman house.

Sabrina sighed. "That's Harvey. Gotta go!" She ran out of the kitchen. A moment later Salem heard the front door slam.

As soon as Sabrina was gone, Salem jumped down from the countertop and took a long, slow stretch as if nothing else mattered in the world. Then he set out on patrol.

Every time he was left alone in the house, Salem made sure to take a tour of all of the places in the kitchen where someone might have left him a snack.

He sniffed carefully at the refrigerator door. Sealed tight. *Drat.* Sometimes one of the aunts left it open enough that he could wedge a paw in, but not today. All the cupboards were closed, as well. Even the garbage had been emptied!

Disappointed, Salem slowly trotted toward his food bowl. Pretty Kitty cat chow tasted like cardboard, no matter what flavor was advertised on the bag—but it was still food, and there was nothing else to eat.

When he had eaten every crumb and

even licked the bowl spotlessly clean, Salem grew very sleepy. He wobbled a little bit as he walked away from the bowl, his tummy stuffed tight as a sausage skin.

He needed an after-breakfast nap, and he needed it *now*. But like all cats, he had to find just the right spot first. He decided that the cushy down comforter on Sabrina's bed would be the perfect place.

Salem headed for the stairs. His feet seemed to get heavier and heavier with each step. The more he thought about it, the more it felt as if Sabrina's bedroom was miles away now.

On the other hand, that patch of sunlight on the living room carpet was only steps away, and it looked mighty inviting.

He made it as far as the foot of the stairs before he decided that, yes indeed, the living room carpet was *almost* as soft as Sabrina's comforter, and it was lots, lots closer.

Salem barely made it to the patch of sunlight before he flopped down and began to snore. His last conscious effort was to roll over on his back so the sun could warm his bulging belly.

Chapter 2

The patch of sunlight had disappeared by the time Salem woke up.

The first thing he noticed was that he was still lying on his back. This was unusual because, like most cats, he preferred sleeping in a curled-up ball, even if he'd started out in another position.

The second thing he noticed was a soft tickling sensation on his upturned belly. Still groggy from overeating, Salem didn't bother to see what was causing the sensation. He just lazily moved to scratch at it with his right rear paw.

That's when he noticed two more strange things. First, his right rear leg wouldn't move. Second, neither would any of his other legs.

Shaking the sleep from his muzzy thoughts, Salem popped open his eyes and stared in shock at two small figures standing on his belly. Mice! Two *mice!* And they were actually *standing* on him!

Feline instincts kicked in and Salem bounded to his feet. Or rather, he tried to. He discovered that the reason his legs wouldn't move was that they were tied with thread. The thread looped around his paws and crisscrossed over his body and somehow attached to the living room carpet. He shot a quick glance at the floor and saw that the threads were held in place by dozens of shiny steel pins. Hilda's sewing kit lay dumped out nearby.

13

Salem couldn't believe it. He'd been ambushed in his sleep by mice!

And very strange mice they were, too. They stood on their hind legs. They also had tiny scraps of red cloth tied around their heads like masks, complete with small eyeholes chewed through them.

The smaller mouse had a length of red handkerchief tied around his neck like a cape. The bigger mouse held a plastic picnic knife between his front paws.

The big mouse pointed the plasticware at Salem when he saw that the cat was awake. "Do you have any final words before your just and horrible punishment?" he hissed.

If Salem was shocked and surprised by finding himself tied down to the floor like Gulliver in the land of Lilliput, he was almost more surprised when the mouse spoke. Talking animals who were transformed witches or magical creatures were common things in the Other Realm, but here in the Mortal Realm, they were unusual. Usually.

The smaller mouse raised the edges of his cape high and proclaimed, "I am the Cheesed Avenger, protector of the weak and guardian of the gouda!" He tried for a booming voice but, being a little mouse, only achieved a soft squeak. "This is my faithful friend, uh . . .uhh . . ." He glanced over at his larger fellow. "Hey, Mort, you never told me what you wanted your hero-name to be."

Mort sighed heavily. "Look, Mikey, I don't want a hero name. I don't need a hero name. I don't need a disguise. I just need to do in the cat."

Mikey was mortified. "You're not supposed to call me Mikey when we're on the job!" he squealed. "Otherwise this vile villain cat will learn our true identities and take revenge on our loved ones!"

15

Mort gritted his mousy teeth in annoyance. "Yo, cheddar-head, there's only you and me—we don't have any loved ones," he hissed. "All the other mice ran away after we ate that funny glowing cheese, remember? Besides, how's pussy-foot here going to take revenge on anybody after we chop him into itty-bitty kittybits?" He waved his plastic knife to make his point.

Salem watched all this, wondering whether he'd gone mad or was still asleep. And then he figured it out. "Very funny, Sabrina!" he called toward the ceiling. "So you cast a spell to give me nightmares if I ate all my food at once. Ha ha. Ha ha."

Mort and Mickey looked at each other in confusion.

"Who's he talking to, Mikey?" Mort asked.

Mikey shrugged. "I dunno, Mort, but

he's not taking his doom very seriously. Think something's wrong with him?"

"There's nothing wrong with me that waking up won't cure," said Salem.

Mikey giggled. "He thinks he's dreaming!"

Mort smiled a wicked smile. "Is *this* a dream, fatball?" He leaped up into the air and landed heavily on Salem's swollen tummy.

"Ook!" blurted Salem, his eyes crossing.

"Or this?" Mikey did a quick foot-stomping dance on Salem's stomach, ending in a series of heavy hops.

"Oog, oog, oog!" Salem grunted. "All right, all right, you win! You're not a dream! You're little mice sent to torment me for eating my food too fast!"

"Food!" the mice gasped together in horror.

Mort shuddered. "Did you hear that,

Mikey? He called poor Moto *food!*" He tossed his friend the plastic knife and hissed, "Cover me!"

Mikey held the blade level as Mort walked across Salem's belly and right up to his face. The mouse's eyes were angry slits behind his little red mask. "I should have known that a villain like you wouldn't give his victims a second thought—but at least give our friend the dignity of remembering his name."

Lying on his back with all four paws tied down, it was hard for Salem to lift his neck up far enough to talk to the mouse. His chin kept bumping into his chest. "Remembering *whose* name?" he demanded.

"My turn, my turn!" Mikey shouted, running up beside his friend. He struck a super-heroic pose with the knife held like a flat sword. "The Cheesed Avenger has declared war against feline oppressors on behalf of his abused and fallen comrades of mousedom!" He pointed a tiny finger at Salem. "You stand accused of the murder of our friend Moto—"

"Our *only* mouse friend since that thing happened with the cheese . . ." Mort broke in.

"Look at his body and tell us how you plead." Mikey pointed at something to the left of Salem's head.

Trying to keep an eye on the plastic knife, Salem looked in the direction that Mikey indicated. Lying on the living room carpet was a gray mouse-shaped object. Its four paws pointed stiffly in the air and a square section of its belly was folded back like a little door.

"Oh, that's my battery-powered electronic Moto-Mouse with Realistic Fur," Salem said in surprise. "I got it from the Sharper Kitty Catalog. Boy, I haven't seen that since it died."

The mice gasped and looked at each other in horror. "He confessed!" squeaked Mort.

"Guilty!" shouted Mikey, waving the knife. "Guilty! Guilty!"

Salem's head snapped back toward them. "It's only a toy," he protested.

"He adds insult to injury!" shrilled Mikey.

Mort crossed his tiny arms and looked sternly at Salem. "Cat, we find you guilty of the murder of Moto-Mouse. Are you ready to suffer your just punishment?"

"Punishment?" sneered Salem. "Right. What do you pipsqueaks think you can do to me?"

With that, Mikey swung the white plastic blade menacingly back and forth in front of Salem's nose. "We're going to do to *you* what you did to our pal Moto!"

Chapter 3

Salem rolled his eyes and groaned. What he'd originally thought was just a bad dream was quickly turning into a real-life nightmare. He could hardly believe that two mad mice—talking mice, no less—had him tied spread-eagled on the floor and were threatening to do something terrible to him. And all this over a battery-operated cat toy!

As quietly as he could, Salem tugged against the threads holding his paws.

There was a tiny bit of slack there, but not enough for him to wriggle free. He watched Mikey swing the plastic knife back and forth, back and forth, and realized that it was time to apply some kitty wit to the situation.

"So," he said casually. "You guys been in the hero business long?"

Both mice looked at each other, then turned back to stare at Salem suspiciously. "No . . ." answered Mort.

Mikey did a quick check of his mask and cape. "Did we do something wrong?"

"No, no," Salem assured them. "I'd say that the fact you got the drop on me so easily shows that you really know your stuff."

Mort looked thoughtful and Mikey looked positively proud at this compliment.

"Well, we did study up," admitted Mort.

"Yeah," added Mikey. "I watched *Mouse Hunter III: Rodent's Revenge* seventeen times while you and the humans were asleep."

Mort patted his friend's head. "Poor Mikey has a permanent flat spot on top of his head from slamming into the rewind button on your VCR," he explained.

Salem nodded to himself. "And here I thought Sabrina kept leaving that movie in the machine just to bug me."

"Nope," said Mikey. "That was us!" He twirled the picnic knife in a series of figure eights like a super-small samurai, *swish-swish-swish!*

"Pretty slick, huh?" Mort said, indicating his friend.

Salem just cocked his head, ignoring the mice for a moment as he sifted through his memory. "You know, in all the years I've been a mouse-chaser, I can't recall ever meeting any mice that fought back like you two. Or any that could talk, for that matter."

"That's because, like all great heroes, we have an Origin," Mort said proudly.

"Wanna hear it?" said Mikey, obviously hoping that Salem would say yes.

Salem was way ahead of him. "Of course," he replied quickly. "Isn't there a rule that says the hero has to explain everything before giving the villain his punishment?"

Of course, Salem really couldn't care less about Mort and Mikey's "Origin." He just had to keep the mice distracted. He had extended a claw from his right paw and was using it to slowly cut one of the threads holding him down.

Mikey happily shifted his picnic knife under one arm, allowing the rounded point to drop to Salem's furry chest as he resumed his heroic mouse-stance.

24

To Salem's relief, the little plastic blade was as dull as he'd thought it would be. He was in no danger. All he had to do was keep the mice busy as he worked on the thread.

"Once," Mikey began, "we were regular mice, just like all the other mice in this house. We hid in the walls by day and hunted for scraps at night."

"That was before the cheese," put in Mort.

Mikey looked upset at the interruption. "Who's telling this story, you or me?"

"We both ate the cheese," Mort insisted.

"Yes, but you're the one who doesn't want a hero-name." Mikey pouted. "Only heroes have Origins, and I'm telling my Origin."

Unnoticed by the arguing mice, the thread snapped silently under Salem's claw. The cat immediately went to work on another thread with the claws of his left paw. "What about the cheese?" he said, to bring the mice back on topic.

"It wasn't like any other cheese we'd ever had," said Mikey. "We found it on the porch. It was green and it glowed in the dark."

"Merlin's Mozzarella!" Salem blurted in surprise. "That explains everything!"

A week before, Zelda Spellman had insisted on having a gourmet dinner, so she'd ordered zap-out food from the Other Realm's nicest restaurant. Along with a tray of the more usual cheeses—Sorcerous Stilton, Enchanted Cheddar, Fantasia Fromage and the like—she'd ordered a piece of the rarest of all witch cheeses, Merlin's Mozzarella. This was a cheese created by the great wizard Merlin. Since it had aged for over fifteen hundred years, it was a perfectly horrible, smelly cheese, but Merlin had made it himself, so nobody had the heart to say anything bad about it.

The Mozzarella had been so strong that Hilda had put it out on the porch so that everyone could enjoy the rest of the dinner. The mice had eaten spoiled magic cheese!

No wonder they were nutsy.

There was a soft twanging sound as the thread holding Salem's left paw suddenly snapped free. He wriggled just a bit and discovered that all of the threads holding him now felt looser. When they'd tied him down, the mice must have simply run back and forth over his body, carrying the spool of thread and looping it over pins stuck into the carpet. How lucky! He was tied down with only one very long thread!

That knowledge made Salem grin. "Great story, guys," he said. "Made me hungry, in fact. Care to stay for a snack, say—*you*?"

27

With that, Salem thrust his head forward, straining against the loose thread across his forehead so that he could snap his teeth at the mice.

"Yeeee!!" wailed Mikey and Mort, scrambling backward in panic and leaping off the angry cat's belly.

There were still enough threads crisscrossing Salem's body so that he couldn't just leap up after the mice. He had to twist back and forth to yank himself free of every loop.

His struggle gave the two mice just enough time to run from the living room and scamper up the stairs.

A low growl rumbled in Salem's throat. As much as he'd acted cool and calm while helpless, he was actually boiling mad at having been outsmarted by mere Mortal-Realm rodents. He raced up the stairs after the mice yelling, "Now you're going to feel my wrath, you rotten rodents!"

He paused when he reached the landing at the top of the stairs. The mice weren't there. Where had they gone? His nose told him that they'd been on the landing, but they'd run around in circles several times, making their tracks confusing.

Salem cocked his ears toward the hallway that led to Hilda's and Zelda's rooms. No sounds came from that direction.

Then he heard soft scratching sounds directly in front of him. They were in Sabrina's bedroom! "Hah!" he muttered to himself. "Got you now, you vindictive little vermin."

Crouching low to the ground, his belly fur scraping along the floor, Salem slunk into Sabrina's room. The two crazy mice were nowhere to be seen, but he could hear them whispering to each other.

He slipped from the doorway to the

space behind the mirror. Then he padded across the floor and ducked under Sabrina's desk. They were close . . . very close. Salem started to creep forward, leaving the shelter of the desk and heading under the chair.

Suddenly a stream of unbelievably smelly liquid poured down on his head, followed by a plastic bottle that bonked against his skull. With a "Yow!" of surprise, Salem jumped straight up. He hit his head on the underside of the chair seat and nearly knocked himself out.

Stunned, he could only stare helplessly through crossed eyes as Mikey and Mort leaped down from the desktop and scrabbled out the door.

Chapter 4

The odor of fruity bubble gum filled Salem's sensitive feline nostrils, blocking out every other sense organ he possessed. He felt nothing, tasted nothing, saw and heard nothing—the universe was just one big noseful of fruity bubble gum.

He let out a yowl of misery. What had those crazy mice done to him?

Slowly his other senses returned. His gaze fell on the plastic bottle with its label, which read Eau de Gumme. It was a sample bottle of perfume that Sabrina had gotten in the mail. "Oh, great," he moaned. "Why isn't there a law against junk mail?"

Now that his other senses had returned, Salem realized that his poor overloaded nose was completely shot. He'd have to depend on his hearing and eyesight to track down the mice.

And oh, how they were going to pay for the humiliation they'd caused him! His mind searched for suitable images of revenge: mouse fritters . . . mouse *à la* mode . . . mouse paté. No, nothing came up that was horrible enough. He'd think of something suitably terrible—*after* he caught them.

He ran down the stairs in search of his tormentors.

One by one Salem checked the first floor for mouse signs. The living room, the sitting room, the dining room, and the hallway were clear. Then, just as he crept into the kitchen, he caught a movement out of the corner of his eye. It was difficult to be sure, but it had looked like a mousy tail disappearing through the cat door between the kitchen and the porch.

In a flash Salem leaped across the kitchen and dived through the flap of the cat door. Once out on the porch he paused, perfectly still, his eyes flicking from the screen door to the plant-covered shelves to Hilda's potting bench. There! Was that the twitch of a mouse tail up by that watering can on the bench? Yes! Something sleek and dark hung over the bench's edge, and Salem detected whispers behind the can.

The cat leaped for the bench, paws, body, and tail stretching to their fullest length, his jaws clamping down on his target before it could twitch away.

He had it!

Good thing, too, because in his haste, Salem had misjudged his jump and left himself nothing to land on. He was already falling back to the floor. But at least he was dragging one of the mice down with him.

At least, that was what he thought. Now, as he fell in what seemed like slow motion, his only thought was this: How could one mouse feel so heavy? And he couldn't help but wonder—mice didn't make the sound of metal scraping on wood, did they?

Salem looked up just in time to realize that he hadn't caught a mouse at all. What he'd thought was a tail was actually a leather shoelace tied around the spout of Hilda's watering can!

As his paws touched down on the floor, he could see two fuzzy little faces peeking over the edge of the bench above, laughing down at him.

And then he got wet.

Chapter 5

Salem just stood there and shivered. He wasn't cold. No, far from it. He was hot with anger and shame. Few creatures in the animal kingdom look as silly as a wet cat, and he knew it.

The liquid pouring from the watering can soaked him from whiskers to tail. Worse, it was an unnatural shade of green. Worse still, it made his skin itch like crazy. Before Salem realized what he was doing, he sat down with a loud *squelch!* sound and, with a hind leg, scratched at his neck, flicking green spray all over his face. What awful stuff had those mice dumped on him?

Luckily there was a label on the watering can. While Hilda was the kind of person who would mix up just any old thing and then hope to remember what it was later, her older sister Zelda insisted on making labels for everything.

Taped to the side of the watering can was a brightly colored label with frills and floral decorations. It read: MARTHA SMUGGEST'S PERFECT PLANT-GRO.

Salem read the words and grimaced. "Great. Now I'll smell like Eau de Gumme by way of the nearest compost pile."

He shook vigorously, flicking off as much of the stuff as he could. Then he headed back through his kitty door, wanting more than ever to do horrible things to Mikey and Mort.

Strange. The cat door was smaller all of a sudden. At least, it felt smaller. Salem could barely squeeze himself through. It was as if something in his fur kept snagging the door edges, giving way with odd little popping sounds. He struggled and pulled, finally pulling himself all the way through and into the kitchen.

He glanced over his shoulder at himself—and howled.

He was covered with flowers! Wherever the Plant-Gro solution had drenched his coat, miniature daisies were sprouting! A circle of happy little daisies was growing around the base of his tail. A clump of daisies stuck out of the fur in the middle of his back. He even had tiny daisies pushing up between his toes!

At this rate, he'd become a walking floral arrangement in minutes!

"Oh, this'll take me hours of grooming to fix," he grumbled. It was bad enough having to bathe himself with his tongue. Now he'd have to weed himself as well.

He glanced about the kitchen, frowning. "You mice are toast!"

With his nose still numb from Eau de Gumme and his ears distracted by the small *pop! pop! pop!* of daisies sprouting on his back, Salem had only his eyes to depend on now.

He scanned the kitchen for signs of the mice. There were snags in the sheer curtains covering the French windows. His eyes traveled upward, following a path of pulled threads.

There they were—scampering about on the molding that ran around the walls just below the ceiling.

How was he supposed to get up there?

Salem tried to think, but it was hard to concentrate with Mort and Mikey giggling and taunting him with, "Daisy cat, daisy cat! Lazy, crazy daisy cat!"

Salem's ears flattened against his head, and his eyes narrowed. So far, the magically amplified mice had beaten every one of his feline instincts. How could he possibly get rid of them? There had to be something he could do!

Then a light dawned in his mind. "That's it!" he murmured. "That's the problem right there!" Of course Mort and Mikey could outthink him—they had *magic* on their side! They'd be able to outthink any cat around.

But Salem wasn't just a cat. He was a witch in a cat's body. His human brain should let him outthink mice any day. And as for magic, well, *he* could find a way to play that game, too.

Salem went to Zelda's and Hilda's spell pantry. Luckily for him, its door wasn't shut tight, unlike all the other cupboards in the kitchen. The pantry was filled with the Spellman witches' collection of magi-

cal ingredients and ready-made spells—
nothing that a cat would normally want.
But today Salem needed some magical
help.

"Open sez me," Salem snarled, sinking
his claws into the wood of the door and
pulling it open. It swung wide to reveal
shelf after shelf of boxes and bottles.

Both Hilda and Zelda were avid bak-
ers, and their prize-winning recipe was
Floating-Upside-Down Cake. The secret
of their batter was a pinch of Montgolfier's Ever-Rise Yeast, which was har-
vested from only the fluffiest clouds in
the Other Realm.

Since Salem didn't have hands, he
couldn't simply open the box of yeast.
He was forced to chew his way through
the cardboard.

He'd planned to make a neat little
hole in one bottom corner of the box,
but the constant mouse-chittering he

could hear in the background made him angry, and he bit down harder than he'd planned.

A cloud of white yeast powder *poofed!* out of the hole and filled his mouth. Even though he coughed most of it back out, Salem still swallowed quite a bit of it.

Its effect was immediate.

Salem felt his stomach swell up. Normally Montgolfier's Ever-Rise Yeast created gas that made baked goods float in the air. In this case, it was filling Salem's tummy with gas, turning him into a kitty-balloon. Slowly he lifted up off the floor, gently rising as the yeast itself rose.

"Mice, prepare to meet your airborne doom!" Salem laughed as he floated ever higher.

He was floating past the Ever-Rise Yeast box when he suddenly noticed the warning printed in big red letters on its side: CAUTION! NEVER EVER USE MORE THAN *ONE* PINCH AT A TIME.

Salem thought of the huge gulp he'd swallowed.

Uh-oh.

Chapter 6

In a flash Salem's gentle rise turned into a rocket launch.

"Hey, Mikey, look!" squealed Mort. "It's the Arbor Day blimp!"

"Do you think he gives rides?" Mikey giggled. "I wanna ride the daisy cat, I wanna ride the daisy cat!"

Salem's back slammed into the ceiling, scattering daisies. The impact made him see double for a moment. "Stand still," he woozily ordered the mice on the molding. "All four of you."

"Ooo, I'm scared," tittered Mort in amusement. "I've never been threatened by a flying floral arrangement before."

"Say, this could be our epic battle," said Mikey. He straightened his mask and whipped his cape around for effect, proclaiming in his deepest voice, "I shall battle for truth, justice, and American cheese against the evil Floating Cat!" He grinned. "This could be a movie, or even a TV show!"

"Yeah," agreed Mort. He could hardly keep from snickering. "Should we hold auditions for the villain, or should we just cast whoever"—he snorted—"whoever *floats* by?"

Both mice collapsed with laughter, almost tumbling from the narrow molding.

Salem felt his cheeks burn red with

embarrassment. Fortunately, his thick black fur hid his blush. No matter how hard he tried to pretend it wasn't true, he knew he'd failed at maintaining the First Law of Cathood: Be Dignified.

Cats have always considered themselves the most dignified creatures on the planet, and Salem was no exception. Yet all the humiliations the mice had caused him were nothing compared to being laughed at. No matter the cost, he was determined to get those mice!

First, however, he had to figure out a way of getting *to* the mice.

Salem wriggled around, trying to see if he might somehow move across the ceiling. He discovered that he could make himself bob up and down by pushing against the ceiling with his head, but he couldn't control in which direction he bobbed. Besides, bobbing around made the mice laugh at him even harder.

45

There had to be a better way to move around. How did spiders manage it? Many times Salem had sprawled on his back on Sabrina's bed watching spiders run around on the ceiling upside-down.

Hey, if spiders could do it, so could a floating cat!

He bumped himself away from the ceiling with his head, but this time he twisted his body so he hit the ceiling paws-up. He sank his claws into the plaster and held tight.

Now this was more like it! With the yeast gas pushing him up and his claws firmly in the ceiling, it was just like walking on the floor—of an upside-down room!

Salem grinned and began to "walk" toward the mice.

Mort was still doubled over with laughter and didn't see Salem approaching. Mikey was the first to notice their danger.

"Yeep!" shrilled Mikey. "Incoming cat at twelve o'clock!"

Salem continued his approach, getting more and more used to spider-walking. He reached one end of the molding quicker than he'd anticipated and blocked off the mice's retreat.

They scrambled over each other and ran along the molding in the opposite direction.

Salem pushed off the wall and bobbed over to that end of the molding, cutting the mice off again. He smiled, showing his fangs. Whichever way the mice went, he'd be able to block their escape.

"Now I've got you!" He laughed.

He'd intended to sound threatening, but that's not what happened. Instead, the pressure of the yeast-gas in his belly escaped a little when he talked, making his words come out in a long, squeaky, "Noooow IIIIII've gotchooooo!"

47

Worse yet, as the gas escaped, Salem suddenly started to sink. Only by digging his claws deep into the ceiling plaster could he keep from falling.

He knew he shouldn't look down, but by reflex, Salem *did* look down. There he was, ten feet above the hard linoleum floor.

It was a long way down.

And when Salem tore his gaze away from the doom awaiting him if he fell, he saw Mort and Mikey leaping through the air—directly at him.

Chapter 7

Mort and Mikey landed square on Salem's gas-bulged belly. For the second time that day, they stared down into their victim's face, and for the second time that day, Salem was powerless to do anything about it.

"He's full of gas," Mort said.

"All we have to do is get it out of him," Mikey added, "and we have instant flat-cat."

With that, the two mad mice began

jumping up and down on Salem's belly. Salem desperately gripped the ceiling with his claws and tried to keep his mouth shut. If he lost all his gas, he'd end up a cat pancake! But what could he do?

Mort pretended that he was skipping rope with an invisible jump rope and sang a made-up song about floating cats.

While Mort skipped and sang, Mikey did his imitation of a Spanish flamenco dancer, swirling his cape around as he stomped on Salem's stomach. *"Olé, olé!"* he yelled as he stomped.

Salem groaned. All this vibration was churning up the Ever-Rise Yeast still in his tummy, making it produce gas in big bubbles instead of at a slow, even rate. On top of that, the mouse dancing was knocking loose clouds of yellow pollen from the daisies sprouting in his coat. The golden dust was billowing into Salem's face and drifting up his nose, making it itch.

It's a little-known fact, but because of the sensitivity of their noses, some cats are as likely to have hay fever as humans are. Lucky Salem! He was one of those cats.

He felt the first sneeze begin as a faint tickle in his left nostril. He could handle a tickle, but it quickly grew into an unbearable itch. He squinched his face around, trying to soothe his nose without touching it. No good. The itch burst out in a short snort.

As sneezes go, it was a little one. But its effect was monstrous. When Salem sneezed, a great bubble of yeast-gas escaped with it.

Zelda Spellman, being a scientist, was fond of lecturing Salem on the laws of science. One of those laws said that for every action, there is an equal and opposite reaction. Hanging upside-down from the ceiling in the Spellman kitchen,

Salem learned firsthand what that law actually meant.

When that little "achoo" left his mouth, the yeast gas accompanied it with such force that it actually propelled Salem backward. His claws, still stuck in the ceiling plaster, left big gouges as they scraped along, and Salem ended up hanging about a foot away from where he'd started.

The mice never suspected that Salem would jerk backward like that. They lost their footing and rolled down the great curve of his belly, almost falling off the cat entirely. Only by grabbing frantically at the daisies did Mort and Mikey keep from plummeting to the floor.

Of course, by shaking the daisies, they released another cloud of pollen that headed straight for Salem's nose.

That was all it took to produce complete disaster.

Salem managed to keep his claws in the plaster during the next sneeze, although he did leave another set of parallel scratches in the ceiling as he blew himself backward.

But as the yeast-gas left him, so did its magical floating power. Without the lifting power of the Ever-Rise yeast, Salem began to get heavier with each sneeze.

As everyone knows, really serious sneezes come on like a hurricane, and there's nothing the poor sneezer can do but weather the storm out.

The third sneeze broke Salem's grip on the ceiling. The fourth and fifth sneezes banged him into the opposite corner of the kitchen like a fancy shot on a pool table.

Salem was so dizzy by now that all he could do was watch the upside-down world fly away backward in front of him as each sneeze jet-propelled him through the air.

53

Mort was terrified. His back paws dug into Salem's fur while his front paws and tail clutched daisies for security.

Mikey, however, was having the time of his life. With his cape flapping behind him, he clung to a daisy. He yelled, "Ride 'em, catboy!" as Salem jerked upside-down through the air.

Each time Salem sneezed out yeast-gas, his altitude gradually dropped. On one hand, this was a good thing—it kept him from banging into the doorway on his ninth sneeze. On the other hand, it was a bad thing—he missed the doorway but zoomed into another room entirely.

This room was filled with two lifetimes of carefully collected knickknacks.

Zelda's tastes ran to fine china. Salem's tenth and eleventh sneezes took him through her collection, turning them into exploded piles of broken clay. He missed her treasured figures of the Nine Muses created in 1737, but made short work of her ruby-red Depression glass.

Hilda's tastes weren't as refined as her sister's. Her collection had a lot of china plates painted with scenes of dogs in human costumes playing card games or plastic toys that came in cereal boxes. Sneeze twelve made most of these collectibles past history.

It was sneeze thirteen that seemed fated to seal Salem's doom.

It was by far the biggest and most violent sneeze he had yet produced. It was so strong, in fact, that it blew away all that itchy pollen from his nose and emptied the last of the Ever-Rise yeast from his innards. Without the lifting power of the yeast gas, Salem headed for the floor.

With his head finally clear, Salem looked past the mice on his belly to see where he was going to land. He moaned at what he saw hurtling toward him.

Set aside in its own display case, on its own special pedestal, was the most valuable thing Hilda owned. Priceless, unique, and irreplaceable, the "Angel Elvis" coin bank was the product of a century-long ceramics class that she had once taken. It was the best thing she'd ever made with her own two hands. It was also the only thing she'd made that didn't look like a wobbly ashtray. Bursting with pride, Hilda had zapped up a special place in the wall to hold her treasure and keep it safe.

Unfortunately, nothing could keep it safe from a backward-flying cat.

Chapter 8

Salem closed his eyes, resigning himself to his doom. "I'm the only cat who's going to spend the rest of his life in the doghouse," he moaned to himself, and waited for the final, deafening, Elvis-wrecking crash.

But instead of a crash, there was a burst of crackling blue light, and Salem found himself hanging frozen in mid-air.

"What in the name of David Copperfield is going on here?" came Sabrina's surprised voice.

Salem tried to answer, but the teenage witch's freeze spell barely let the cat breathe, much less talk. With great effort, he rolled his eyes around far enough to see Sabrina standing in the doorway between the dining room and the living room.

Her eyes grew wide as she noticed Mort and Mikey clinging to the cat's fur. "Are those mice, Salem?" she asked in disbelief. "You made all this mess playing with *mice*?"

"Mmm mm mmmph!" Salem replied.

Sabrina scowled at his grunted answer, then grinned as she realized her mistake. "Sorry," she blurted, and zapped Salem's mouth free.

"I said, I wasn't playing, I was doing my job," Salem snapped.

Sabrina waved a hand to indicate all

the mess in the room. "Since when has your job description included trashing everything my aunts hold dear?"

Reminded of Zelda and Hilda's wrath-to-come, Salem broke into desperate sobs. "It wasn't my fault!" he cried. "It was those muh-muh-mice! They made me do it! They tied me down! They dumped bubble-gum perfume on me! They *laughed* at me! Whuh-huh-huh . . ."

For a moment Sabrina actually felt pity for the poor cat. Then the huge mess grabbed her attention again. "And just how did two tiny mice get the better of a full-grown cat?" she demanded.

Salem blinked and, quick as a wink, changed the subject. "So what brings you home so early?" he asked. "Did you bring me lunch?"

Sabrina's eyes twinkled with merriment. "Mr. Kraft didn't think to bring a clothespin for his nose," she said. "When

59

the wind changed direction at the farm, he was suddenly very sorry he'd taken a decongestant to cure his head cold. It was the shortest field trip in the history of Westbridge High School." She fanned her hand in front of her face as if swishing away a horrible stench. "It was like a wish come true."

"Speaking of having wishes granted," Salem said grumpily, "how about taking this freeze spell off me?" He glared at the flowers growing out of his fur. "I have a long afternoon of grooming and weeding ahead of me."

Sabrina had been so distracted by quizzing Salem about the cause of all the mess that she'd totally forgotten that the cat was still hovering upside-down in midair. She dissolved the freeze spell and was about to lower Salem to the floor when a shrill little voice called to her from Salem's belly.

"Are you pro-mouse or anti-mouse?" Mikey demanded as he and Mort climbed up on Salem's stomach to face her.

"Are *these* the mice who caused you so much trouble, Salem? They're so *cute!*" Sabrina gushed. "Those little masks are just *darling*."

"Pardon me if I don't join you in the mouse-appreciation celebration," Salem sneered. "These little mice are the cause of all my problems."

"Only because you murdered poor Moto!" Mikey replied hotly.

"I keep telling you cheese-heads—it's only a battery-operated toy!" Salem howled.

"Oppressor!" shouted Mikey.

"Feline chauvinist!" yelled Mort.

Sabrina froze everyone again just to get a moment of silence. She walked into the living room and came back dangling the electronic mouse by its tail. "Is this

what all the trouble was about?" she asked.

"Mmmmph!" the three animals agreed in unison.

Sabrina raised an eyebrow and looked sternly at Salem, Mikey, and Mort. "If I fix . . . uh, Moto here, will you three promise to stop fighting and help clean up this mess?"

Salem and the mice glared at each other for a moment. "Mmm-hmm," they finally said together.

Sabrina zapped a fresh battery into Moto's belly and closed up the hatch. Immediately the toy's eyes glowed red and his motors started whirring. She set it down on the floor, where it began scurrying around in a wide circle.

"Mmmmghflpt!" Mikey and Mort crowed, overjoyed at seeing their friend healthy and active again.

*　　*　　*

Sabrina sat at the dining room table piecing together shards of broken china. Whenever she found two edges that fit, her magic bonded them together seamlessly. She mended the last crack in Zelda's ruby-red Depression glass and floated it back to its proper place on the buffet.

Salem jumped up on the table and dropped another china shard from his mouth in front of Sabrina. "I still don't understand why we can't stop for a little snack," he complained. "These pieces are so dusty I could use a drink of water—or a can of really moist tuna."

"We'll all have a snack when everything is cleaned up and mended," Sabrina told him sternly. "If you had any control over your appetite, none of this would have happened. Now go tell Mort and Mikey to stop watching Moto and find all the pieces of Aunt Hilda's disco dishes next."

Salem stared snootily at the two masked mice who were watching their electronic friend race around in tight figure eights. "I still don't think it's fair," Salem huffed. "Since all this was Moto's fault, he should do his share of the work."

Sabrina laughed so hard she nearly broke a plate herself.

Cat Care Tips

1. Some cats love to be brushed, others hate it. You do not need to brush your cat unless it is a longhair cat who develops mats.

2. Healthy cats do not need baths. They clean themselves very well. Baths are very stressful to cats and should be avoided unless otherwise instructed by your veterinarian.

3. Cats should be handled gently—do not squeeze them too tightly when you hug them. Never pull on their tails.

—Laura E. Smiley, MS, DVM, Dipl. ACVIM
Gwynedd Veterinary Hospital

Like another purrr-fect read? Why not check out Salem's next adventure.
Remember – he's a moggy with a mission!

#14 Mascot Mayhem

When Salem's clumsiness helps the Westbridge football team finally win a game, the players agree: Salem will be their new mascot. At first, Salem is satisfied with his new status. The team's on a winning streak, and everyone thinks that Salem is Westbridge's lucky charm.

But Salem gets used to the pampered life and wants even more prestige, so he angles to become the new mascot for a local college. Unfortunately for Salem, the team's current mascot, a bulldog, doesn't want to retire – especially for a cat replacement.

Missed out on Salem's action-packed past?
Why not check out Salem's next adventure.

#12 Rulin' The School

When Salem plays one too many pranks, the Witches'
Council ships him off to obedience school in the Other Realm
for three whole weeks! The school isn't as bad as Salem
feared — it's worse! The cat-hating witch of a vice principal
is out to get him, the greyhound bullies get their laughs by
stuffing Salem into lockers, and worst of all, he's an outcast
who has to eat lunch all by himself.

But then Salem meets Smitty, a geeky grey tabby cat who
just happens to be a computer whiz. Together they come up
with a foolproof plan to escape . . . and teach the whole
school a lesson!